Here's what kids have to say to
Mary Pope Osborne, author of
the Magic Tree House series:

If you didn't make the Magic Tree House Books I would go nuts!!!!—Anthony

Jack gave me the idea of getting a notebook myself.—Reid K.

I hope that you make more Magic Tree House books. They bring magic to my life.
—Michelle R.

You gave me the courage to read. Thanks!
—Lydia K.

I like your books because they are very exciting. It's like I'm traveling around the world with Jack and Annie.—Elizabeth C.

Our imaginations are soaring thanks to you!
—Julie M.

Your books inspired me to read, read, read!
—Eliza C.

Reading your books gave me the idea to write a book myself.—Tyler

I think your books are great. I can't sleep without reading one.—Leah Y.

Teachers and librarians love
Magic Tree House books, too!

Your stories have been a very special part of every day in our class for the last two years. I read aloud to the class each day and we choose someone who gets to be "Jack/Annie," complete with backpack, glasses and journal. We have props from every book. . . . The children act out what is going on.—L. Horist

Introducing my students to your books is the best thing I've done. . . . Jack and Annie have incredibly helped my students' growth in reading.—D. Boyd

Thank you for these great books. They truly "light the fire within" that helps motivate students to read. I enjoy them myself!—D. Chatwin

It is refreshing as a classroom teacher to be able to use such interesting, informational adventure books to motivate and encourage good reading habits.—R. Trump

You have created a terrific tool for motivating children to learn about historical moments and places.—L. George

As a teacher I love how easily your books tie in with curriculum studies. Science and Social Studies units can easily be supplemented using your series. . . . Your books let my students experience other places and times beyond their front door.—T. Gaussoin

Due to your wide variety of settings, my students are learning an invaluable amount of information about history and the world around them, sometimes without even realizing it.—L. Arnts

It amazes me how these books easily lured my students into wanting to read.—T. Lovelady

Dear Readers,

When I did research for Thanksgiving on Thursday, I learned something I hadn't known before. I learned that what we generally think of as the first Thanksgiving—the 1621 feast with the Pilgrims and the Wampanoag people of Plymouth Bay—was not a day set aside to give thanks. It was a three-day festival to celebrate a good harvest. During that time, the Pilgrims and Wampanoag shared many meals. Even so, we traditionally think of this harvest festival as the first Thanksgiving. More than two hundred years later, in 1863, President Abraham Lincoln designated the last Thursday in November as America's national day of Thanksgiving.

I love doing the research for Magic Tree House books because I always learn something new. I hope you'll learn lots of new things, too, when you visit the "first Thanksgiving" with Jack and Annie.

All my best,

Mary Pope Osborne

MAGIC TREE HOUSE® #27

Thanksgiving on Thursday

by Mary Pope Osborne

illustrated by Sal Murdocca

A STEPPING STONE BOOK™

Random House New York

For Bill, LuAnn, Mickey, and Alan—
Thanksgiving friends for many years

Published in the United States by Random House Children's Books, a division of Random House, Inc., New York, and simultaneously in Canada by Random House of Canada Limited, Toronto.

www.randomhouse.com/magictreehouse

Library of Congress Cataloging-in-Publication Data
Osborne, Mary Pope.
Thanksgiving on Thursday / by Mary Pope Osborne ; illustrated by Sal Murdocca.
— 1st ed. p. cm.—(Magic tree house ; #27) "A stepping stone book."
SUMMARY: Jack and Annie travel in their magic tree house to the year 1621, where they celebrate the first Thanksgiving with the Pilgrims and Wampanoag Indians in the New Plymouth Colony.
ISBN 0-375-80615-6 (trade) — ISBN 0-375-90615-0 (lib. bdg.)
[1. Thanksgiving Day—Fiction. 2. Pilgrims (New Plymouth Colony)—Fiction. 3. Plymouth (Mass.)—History—17th century—Fiction. 4. Time travel—Fiction.]
I. Murdocca, Sal, ill. II. Title. PZ7.081167 Th 2002 [Fic]—dc21 2002010907
Printed in the United States of America First Edition
10 9 8 7 6 5 4

Random House, Inc. New York, Toronto, London, Sydney, Auckland

Contents

Prologue

One summer day in Frog Creek, Pennsylvania, a mysterious tree house appeared in the woods.

Eight-year-old Jack and his seven-year-old sister, Annie, climbed into the tree house. They found that it was filled with books.

Jack and Annie soon discovered that the tree house was magic. It could take them to the places in the books. All they had to do was point to a picture and wish to go there. While they are gone, no time at all passes in Frog Creek.

Along the way, Jack and Annie discovered that the tree house belongs to Morgan le Fay. Morgan is a magical librarian of Camelot, the long-ago kingdom of King Arthur. She travels through time and space, gathering books.

Jack and Annie have many exciting adventures helping Morgan and exploring different times and places. In Magic Tree House Books #25–28, they will learn the art of magic. . . .

1

What Feast?

"Come on," said Annie. She stood in the doorway to Jack's bedroom. "Let's check the woods."

"But it's Thursday," said Jack. "We're going to Grandmother's soon."

"I know," said Annie. "But I have a feeling the tree house might be back. I think Morgan might have sent us a new rhyme."

Jack trusted Annie's feelings.

"Okay, but we'll have to be quick," he said.

He threw his notebook and pencil into his backpack. He followed her downstairs.

"Be back soon!" Jack called to their parents.

"*Very* soon!" their dad said.

"Don't forget—it's Thursday," said their mom. "We're leaving for Grandmother's at nine!"

"I know!" said Jack.

"We'll be back in ten minutes!" said Annie.

They hurried out of their house. They ran across their yard and up their street and into the Frog Creek woods.

Jack and Annie ran through light and shadow, until they stopped under the tallest oak.

"Yay!" said Annie.

"You were right!" said Jack.

High in the tree was the magic tree house.

Jack grabbed the rope ladder and started up. Annie was right behind him.

They climbed into the tree house. Sunlight slanted in through the window.

"Good, our gifts from our last trips are still here," said Annie.

She pointed to the scrolls from Shakespeare's theater and the twig from the gorillas.

"Proof we found the magic of the theater and the magic of animals," said Jack.

"Look," said Annie. She pointed to a book lying in a dark corner. A piece of paper was sticking out of it.

Jack pulled out the paper.

"It's from Morgan," he said.

He read:

Dear Jack and Annie,

Good luck on your third journey to find a special magic. This rhyme will guide you:

To find a special magic,
When work and toil are done,
Gather all together,
Turn three worlds into one.

Thank you,
Morgan

"So who do we gather with?" wondered Jack.

Annie held up the book. The painting on the cover showed a basket of corn on a wooden table. The title said *A Feast to Remember*.

"We gather at a feast," she said. She pointed to the cover. "I wish we could go there."

"Hold on," said Jack. "What kind of feast? Where and *when*?"

But the wind had started to blow.

The tree house started to spin.

It spun faster and faster.

Then everything was still.

Absolutely still.

2

Shh!

Jack opened his eyes. Bright, golden sunlight poured into the tree house. The air felt crisp and cool.

Annie was wearing a long dress, a white cap, and an apron.

Jack wore a jacket with a frilly collar. He wore short pants, long socks, leather shoes, and a hat. His backpack was now a leather bag.

"I like your hat," said Annie. "It's funny."

"Yours, too," said Jack.

"You look like a Pilgrim," said Annie.

"So do you," said Jack. "Oh, man. I bet we're in the time of the *Pilgrims*!"

He and Annie scrambled to the window.

The tree house had landed in a tall oak near the edge of a forest. Red and yellow leaves rattled in the cool breeze. Past the forest was a small village and past the village was the ocean.

"It *looks* like where the Pilgrims lived," said Jack. "We studied it in school."

He opened the research book and found a picture of the village by the sea. He read aloud:

In 1620, a group of 102 passengers sailed from England to America on a ship called the *Mayflower*. Many of

the people on board wanted freedom of religion. They wanted to worship God in their own way—not the way the king of England made them. Others wanted to find a new life in a new land. Today, we call *all* the people who sailed on the *Mayflower* Pilgrims.

"*Yes!*" said Annie.

Jack read on:

The Pilgrims wanted to settle near New York. But a storm blew their ship north. They landed in a bay on the coast of what is now Massachusetts. Six years before, Captain John Smith had explored the coast. He had named the bay Plymouth.

"Plymouth?" said Annie. "That's where the first Thanksgiving was!"

"Oh, man . . ." Jack smiled. "So *that's* the feast."

"Wow," said Annie. "My class put on a play about the first Thanksgiving."

"Mine, too," said Jack.

"I played Priscilla," said Annie.

"I played a turkey," said Jack.

"Now we'll get to meet the *real* Priscilla!" said Annie. "And Squanto! And Governor Bradford and Miles Standish! Come on!"

She started down the ladder.

"Wait. What will we say?" asked Jack.

"We'll just tell them hi and stuff," said Annie.

"Are you nuts?" said Jack. He put the book into his bag. "They won't understand who we are! We need a *plan*."

He slung the bag over his shoulder and hurried down the ladder after Annie.

"Listen, we need—" Jack started.

"I know, a *plan,*" said Annie. "But first let's get closer to the village and just watch."

"Okay," said Jack, "but we can't let anyone see us. We have to be careful and quiet."

He and Annie started walking carefully through the woods. But they did not walk *quietly*. The autumn leaves crunched and crackled under their leather shoes.

"Shh!" said Jack.

"I can't help it," said Annie. "You're doing it, too!"

"Then we have to stop," said Jack. "Let's get behind that tree and watch from there."

They crunched over to a tree at the edge of the woods. In the distance was a row of small log houses with steep thatched roofs.

Jack pulled out the book. He found the part about the village. Then he pushed his glasses up and read to himself:

> **The Pilgrims brought chickens, geese, goats, and sheep from England. They brought seeds to plant, and they knew how to make traps to catch wild animals for food. But they could not have survived without the help of a Wampanoag (wom-puh-NO-ag) Indian named Squanto. Squanto taught them how to grow corn.**

"Hi, you," Annie whispered. Jack looked up.

Annie was talking to a skinny yellow dog. The dog was sniffing a tree near them.

"Don't let him see us," Jack whispered.

"Why?" said Annie.

The dog looked at them and barked.

"*That's* why!" said Jack.

The skinny dog barked again and again.

Two Pilgrim men ran from the other side of the houses. Then more Pilgrims appeared. They all looked in the direction of the barking dog.

"Oh, no!" said Jack. "Let's go back! We don't have a plan yet!"

He packed up his book and started away from the tree. Suddenly something tightened around his ankle. A tree branch snapped.

"AHHH!" Jack shouted as he was jerked up into the air.

3

Wow?

"Jack!" cried Annie.

The skinny dog barked and jumped around happily.

Jack was hanging a few feet off the ground, with a rope around his ankle. His glasses and hat and bag had fallen to the ground. Jack felt the blood rushing to his head.

"I must have stepped into a hunting trap," he said in a strangled voice.

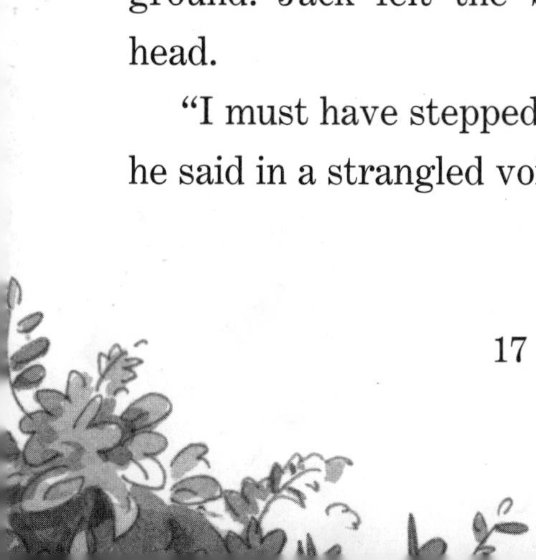

"I'll free you," Annie said. She tried to reach the rope, but it was too high.

Jack heard voices over the wild barking of the dog. A blur of people gathered around him and Annie.

"Oh, mercy!" a woman cried.

"We have caught a boy!" a man said.

The dog licked Jack's face.

"Help," said Jack.

A burly man shooed the dog away, then grabbed Jack. Another cut the rope with a knife. Then they gently lowered Jack to the ground.

Jack sat in the leaves, feeling dizzy. He took the rope off his foot and rubbed his ankle.

"Here," said Annie, handing Jack his glasses, hat, and bag.

He put them all on and stood up. *Now*

he could see. About forty or fifty Pilgrims—men, women, and lots of children—stared at him and Annie. Some of the children were laughing.

The girls were dressed just like the women. The boys were dressed just like the men.

One person, though, looked different from everyone else in the crowd. His skin was brown. A deer skin hung over his shoulder.

His black hair was braided and had a feather in it.

Is that Squanto? Jack wondered. *The Wampanoag Indian who helped out the Pilgrims?*

Two Pilgrim men stepped forward. One had a smile on his face. The other was frowning.

"Good day!" the friendly-looking man said. "Who art thou?"

"I'm Annie," said Annie. "This is my brother, Jack. We come in peace."

"Welcome to Plymouth Colony," said the man. "I am Governor Bradford. This is Captain Standish."

Captain Standish kept frowning. He carried a long gun over his shoulder.

"Oh, wow!" said Annie.

"*Wow?*" said Captain Standish.

"*Wow?*" whispered others, as if they didn't understand.

"I've just heard a lot about you," said Annie. She looked around. "Is Priscilla here?"

"Shhh!" whispered Jack.

"I am Priscilla," said a young woman. She looked about seventeen or eighteen. Her face looked weary, and her eyes were sad.

"Hi," said Annie shyly. "I was you."

"*Annie,*" warned Jack.

"Thou was me?" Priscilla asked. She sounded puzzled.

"Never mind my sister," said Jack. "She's nuts."

"*Nuts?*" repeated Priscilla.

"*Nuts?*" whispered others.

"Oh, brother," said Jack, with a nervous laugh.

"*Oh, brother?*" repeated Priscilla.

Annie giggled.

"Um. Never mind," said Jack. "That's just how we say things at home."

"And where *is* thy home?" Captain Standish asked. He didn't sound as friendly as Governor Bradford or Priscilla.

"Um, we live in a village up north," said Jack. "Our parents sent us here to, uh"—he remembered something from their research book—"to learn how to grow corn."

"But how and when did your family come to America?" the captain asked.

Jack was worried. Now that he had started making up a story, he couldn't back out. Luckily, he remembered something else from their book.

"We sailed to America with Captain John Smith," he said, "when he was exploring the coast. Annie and I were babies then."

"Ah, indeed?" said Governor Bradford.

Jack nodded. "Indeed," he said.

"I believe Squanto knew Captain John Smith when he was in Plymouth," said Captain Standish. "Perhaps he remembers thee."

Everyone in the crowd turned to the man with the braid.

Oh, no! thought Jack. He knew Squanto wouldn't remember them.

"These children say they sailed with Captain John Smith," Governor Bradford said to Squanto. "Does thou remember two wee babes named Jack and Annie?"

Squanto moved closer to Jack and Annie. He looked carefully at their faces. Jack held his breath. His heart pounded.

Squanto turned to the governor.

"Yes," he said quietly. "I remember."

4

We Fish!

Annie grinned. "Good day, Squanto!" she said.

"Good day, Annie," said Squanto. He smiled at her and Jack.

Jack was too surprised to speak. *Why did Squanto say he remembers us?* he wondered. *Is he mistaking us for two other kids?*

Captain Standish looked surprised, too. But Governor Bradford smiled warmly.

"'Tis a wonder," he said. "We welcome all

the small folk sent to us. Children are a gift from God—no matter where they come from."

That's a nice way of looking at things, Jack thought.

Just then, a boy ran up. "Chief Massasoit is here with ninety men!" he shouted.

The boy pointed to a long line of men walking down a path near a cornfield.

Chief Massasoit walked ahead of the others. His face was painted red. He wore a fur robe and white beads.

Governor Bradford, Captain Standish, and Squanto went to meet the visitors.

"Mercy!" a Pilgrim woman whispered.

All the Pilgrims looked worried.

"Art thou afraid?" Annie asked.

"Oh, no," said Priscilla. "We invited Chief

Massasoit and his men to our harvest feast. But we did not expect so many. We have not prepared enough food."

Governor Bradford and Squanto spoke to the chief. Then Squanto led a number of men into the woods. And the governor walked back to the Pilgrims.

"The Wampanoag men will hunt more deer," he said. "But we must also bring more food to the table. Priscilla, please tell the young folk what they must do."

The grown-ups went back to the village as the Pilgrim kids gathered around Priscilla. She told some to carry water or set up tables. She told others to gather vegetables or hunt small animals.

Once the kids were given their jobs, they rushed off to do them. Finally only Jack,

Annie, and a small girl holding a big basket were left.

"Jack, would thou like to go fowling with the boys?" Priscilla asked him. She pointed to a group of boys who had just headed off with the dog.

Jack stared at her in panic. *What does she mean?* he wondered.

"What's 'fowling'?" Annie asked.

"Thou does not know?" said the little girl. "'Tis hunting water birds, of course."

"Jack doesn't know how to do that," said Annie.

"'Tis true? How does thou eat and live?" the little girl asked curiously.

"We, uh . . ." Jack froze.

"We catch—fish!" said Annie.

We do? thought Jack.

“Ah, good!” said Priscilla. “Then I bid thee bring back as many eels and clams as thou can. We have near one hundred fifty mouths to feed.” Priscilla took the basket from the small girl and gave it to Annie.

“We will see thee later!” Priscilla said,

waving. “Mary and I must go help with the cooking.”

“Um . . . ?” said Jack.

But before he could ask any questions, Priscilla and the little girl started back to the village.

5

Eels and Clams

Jack looked at Annie.

"We can't stay here," he said.

"What?" she said. "We can't go home now. The Pilgrims need us to help them."

"But we don't know how to do anything!" Jack said. "And Squanto is going to figure out he doesn't really know us. And—"

"Don't worry so much," said Annie. "We help Mom and Dad make our Thanksgiving dinner every year, don't we? We can help the Pilgrims. But we'd better hurry!"

Clutching the big basket, she started running toward the bay. Jack sighed, then ran after her.

At the rocky shore, they stopped and looked around. Little waves rolled onto the short stretch of sand. The salty air felt clean and fresh. Seagulls swooped over the water.

"I wonder where the eels are?" said Annie. "And the clams?"

"I'll look in the book," said Jack.

He pulled out their book and looked up *eels* in the index. He turned to the right page and read aloud:

> **Squanto showed the Pilgrims a way to catch eels. He showed them how to push the eels out of the wet sand with their bare feet, then grab them with their hands.**

"That sounds fun!" said Annie. She put

down her basket and pulled off her shoes and stockings. She held up her long skirt with one hand. Then she walked over the rocks to the edge of the water.

Jack put the research book into his bag. He pulled off his shoes and stockings and joined Annie.

They dug their bare feet into the wet sand.

"I don't feel anything," said Jack.

"Let's wade into the water," said Annie.

Together they stepped forward.

"Brrr!" said Annie.

"No kidding!" said Jack with a shiver.

He kept squishing the muddy sand with his toes. He felt pebbles and shells. Then he felt something soft.

"Hey, I think I found one," he said.

Annie splashed over to him. "Where?"

“Stand back,” he said. “Here.”

Jack squished harder with his feet. The soft thing moved! Jack squished more. An eel slithered through the water.

Jack grabbed it with both hands!

“AHH!” he yelled.

The eel was long and skinny like a snake. It felt slimy and icky! It twisted and squirmed. Annie laughed as Jack tried to hold on to it.

The eel wiggled out of Jack's hands and fell against Annie.

"Yikes!" she yelled, jumping away and bumping into Jack.

With more screams, they both tumbled into the cold water.

They scrambled up and splashed back to shore. Annie was still laughing.

"Poor eel!" she said, trying to catch her breath. "We scared him half to death!"

"Him?" said Jack.

"F-forget eels," said Annie, her teeth chattering. "What about c-clams?"

Jack was wet and cold. But he took out the book again and looked up *clams*. He turned to the right page and read aloud:

> **Squanto taught the Pilgrims how to dig for quahog (KO-hog) clams. Quahog clams are hard-shell clams. They can live for sixty years or more. The oldest have been known to live for almost 100 years. They—**

"Oh, forget it," Annie broke in.

"What?" said Jack.

"We can't catch *them,*" she said. "They live to be so old. We can't just end their lives."

Jack sighed. He sat down on a rock. Annie sat next to him. Their clothes were soaking wet. Their feet were caked with muddy sand. Their basket was empty.

"What other things do Pilgrim kids do to help?" said Annie.

Jack opened the book again. He looked up *Pilgrim children.* He read aloud:

Pilgrim children worked very hard. They built fences and cared for animals. They planted, harvested, and ground corn. They picked pumpkins, peas, and beans. They guarded the fields. They fished and hunted. They carried water. They collected nuts. They cooked and cleaned. They did everything they were told. They never complained about being tired.

"Oh, man, I feel tired just *reading* this," said Jack, closing the book. "We make lousy Pilgrim children."

"Yeah, I know," said Annie. "Maybe we could do something like . . . like keep an eye on the turkey and tell them when it's ready. That's how I help Mom every year."

"Annie, Thanksgiving in Frog Creek is a

whole different story from Thanksgiving with the Pilgrims," said Jack.

"Annie! Jack!" a voice called.

Jack quickly put away their book. Then they turned around.

Priscilla was standing on a rock. She held a pumpkin and carried a basket filled with yellow squash and red corn.

"I was looking for you," she said.

6

Good Work

"Good day, Priscilla!" said Annie.

"Good day," said Priscilla. She walked to them. "Did thou fill the basket with eels and clams?"

"Not really," said Jack.

"The eel didn't want to get caught," said Annie. "And the clams live to be so old! We didn't think it was right to take their lives."

Priscilla laughed. Her sad eyes sparkled.

"What strange children," she said. "But you

both look wet and cold. Would you like to come to my house and warm up by the fire?"

"Yes!" said Jack and Annie.

They washed off their feet and pulled on their shoes and stockings. Jack picked up his bag. Annie picked up their empty basket.

"Would thou like to put some of my corn and squash in thy basket?" said Priscilla.

"Oh, thanks!" said Annie. She took some corn and squash from Priscilla's basket.

"And perhaps thou would like to carry the pumpkin?" Priscilla said to Jack.

"Sure!" said Jack.

"*Sure?*" said Priscilla.

"I mean, indeed," said Jack. He felt relieved. Now they wouldn't have to go back empty-handed.

Jack wrapped his arms around the heavy

pumpkin. Annie carried the basket. They followed Priscilla back to the village.

The Pilgrims and Wampanoag were gathering in a wide dirt street. Women were baking bread in an outdoor oven. Some boys were setting wooden planks on barrels to make tables. Mary, the little girl, was carrying a bucket of water.

Squanto sat smoking a pipe with Chief Massasoit, Governor Bradford, and Captain Standish.

Jack hoped Mary wouldn't ask him about the clams and eels. He hoped Squanto wouldn't ask him about Captain John Smith. He hoped the governor and the captain wouldn't ask him about home. Jack hid his face behind the fat pumpkin.

Priscilla opened the door to a small house. Then she led Jack and Annie into a dark, smoky room. The only light came from one window and a fire.

"Sit by the hearth," said Priscilla, "so your clothes can dry."

"Where's the hearth?" Annie asked, looking around.

Priscilla laughed again, shaking her head. "There, where the fire lies," she said.

Jack put down the pumpkin and his bag. Annie put down her basket. The hearth was so large, Jack could have stood in it. He and Annie got as close as they could to the warm, crackling fire.

Several pots hung over the fire. Near the pots, a turkey was roasting on an iron rod.

"The Thanksgiving turkey," whispered Annie.

"Cool," said Jack. *The very first Thanksgiving turkey*, he thought.

"Would thou please stir the corn pudding whilst thou art drying?" asked Priscilla. She pointed to one of the pots.

"Indeed," said Jack.

Priscilla took a wooden spoon out of a jug of water near the hearth. She gave it to Jack. He put it into the thick, bubbly pudding and stirred.

"I must gather nuts," said Priscilla. "Whilst I am gone, move the roots close to the ashes and stir herbs into the seafood chowder."

"Indeed," said Annie.

After Priscilla left, Annie looked at Jack.

"What are 'roots' and 'herbs'?" she asked.

"Look in the book," said Jack.

Annie took the research book from Jack's bag. She looked up *roots* and read aloud:

> **The Pilgrims called certain vegetables *roots*. These vegetables, such as carrots and turnips, grow under the ground.**

"Ah!" said Jack. He picked up some carrots and turnips near the hearth and moved them close to the hot ashes.

Next, Annie looked up *herbs*. She read aloud:

The Pilgrims called leafy vegetables that grow above the ground *herbs*. They made salads with herbs. They used dried herbs to flavor soups and seafood chowders.

Jack saw some dried plants hanging from the rafters.

"Those must be the herbs," he said.

Annie broke off a leaf and sniffed it.

"Mmm, that smells good," she said. She leaned close to one of the pots. "And that must be the seafood chowder. It smells like the ocean."

She crumbled the leaf into the chowder. She took another spoon from the jug of water. She and Jack both stirred pots.

“Good work!” Priscilla said as she stepped back into the room.

Jack smiled. The fire had made him hot and sweaty. The smoke burned his eyes. But he didn’t mind. *Finally* he felt useful.

Priscilla put some walnuts close to the fire.

“Squanto taught us which nuts are good to eat,” she said.

“Squanto taught thee a lot,” said Annie.

“He saved our lives,” Priscilla said quietly. “Last winter we were cold and hungry. Half our people died.”

Annie gasped. “How?” she said.

“Sickness,” said Priscilla. “Fever took my mother, my father, and my brother.” Her eyes were bright with tears.

No one spoke. The sound of the crackling

fire filled the room. Then Annie put her arm around Priscilla.

"We're so sorry," said Annie.

"Yes, we are," said Jack.

"Thank you," Priscilla said with a sad smile. "'Twas a terrible winter. But we never gave up hope. And now, God be praised, we have had a good harvest, and we have peace with our neighbors."

In the glow of the firelight, Priscilla was beautiful, Jack thought. Not only was she kind, but she was incredibly brave as well.

"Come," she said. She wiped her eyes and stood up. "Something special is about to take place. Would thou like to watch?"

"Sure! I mean, *indeed!*" said Annie.

She and Jack jumped up and followed Priscilla outside.

7

Arm Exercises

Priscilla led Jack and Annie away from the village toward a large field. The Pilgrims and Wampanoag men had already gathered there.

Jack could hear the beat of a drum. But he couldn't see what was going on.

"Make haste or we will miss it!" said Priscilla.

"Miss what?" asked Annie.

"Captain Standish is about to lead the men and boys," said Priscilla. "They will exercise their arms."

Why do they exercise their arms? Jack wondered. *Will they expect me to join in?*

As he hurried after Priscilla toward the crowd, Jack practiced. He stretched his arms out wide. He made circles in the air. Then he flapped his arms up and down.

Priscilla caught sight of him.

"What art thou doing, Jack?" she asked.

"Exercising my arms," he said.

Priscilla smiled. Then she started to laugh. She laughed and laughed.

So did Jack, but he wasn't sure why.

A loud *BANG!* came from the field.

Jack jumped. He stopped laughing.

A puff of smoke rose into the air. As the crowd parted, Jack saw the Pilgrim men and boys proudly holding up their long guns.

"What just happened?" said Annie.

"The men fired their muskets," said Priscilla. "On special occasions they like to show off their arms."

Oh! thought Jack. *Now I get it! The long guns are muskets, which are also called arms. So "exercising arms" means firing muskets!*

Jack blushed. *Priscilla must think I'm an idiot,* he thought.

But she just smiled at him fondly.

"I thank thee for making me laugh, Jack," she said. "I have not laughed hard in a long time."

Jack shrugged, as if he had meant to make her laugh.

"It is time now to serve our feast," said Priscilla. "I must help with the bread."

"What can we do?" asked Jack.

"Return to my home," said Priscilla, "take the turkey off the spit, put it on a platter, and bring it to a table."

"Oh, great, we get to help with the turkey!" said Annie. "I *always* help with the turkey at home."

"Good," said Priscilla. "May thou feel *my* home is *thy* home today."

Jack was excited, too. He and Annie were

about to serve the *first* turkey at the *first* Thanksgiving! They ran back to the smoky house and rushed inside.

"Where's the platter?" said Jack, looking around. He saw a flat wooden block. "That must be it."

Annie picked up the wooden platter. "How do we get the turkey on it?" she asked.

They moved close to the fire and stared at the turkey roasting on the iron rod.

"That must be the spit," said Jack. The spit sat on iron legs. It had a handle.

Jack pushed his glasses into place. "I'll lift the spit," he said. "Then we'll push the turkey onto the platter."

"Be careful," said Annie.

Jack reached out and wrapped his fingers around the handle of the iron spit.

"OWW!" he shouted. The handle was super hot! He yanked his hand away and knocked the spit off its legs.

The turkey fell into the fire. The grease from the turkey sputtered and popped. The turkey burst into flame! The fire roared!

"AHH!" yelped Jack and Annie together. They jumped back from the hearth.

Jack grabbed the water pot on the floor. He threw the water into the fire. The fire sizzled and smoke billowed up. When the smoke cleared, the fire was out.

But the turkey was completely black.

8

The Feast

Jack buried his face in his hands.

"I don't believe it," he said. "I just burned up the Pilgrims' turkey!"

"Stay calm," said Annie. "I'll get Priscilla."

"No, don't tell Priscilla," moaned Jack.

"We have to tell Priscilla," said Annie.

She hurried out of the house.

Jack lifted his head and stared at the burned turkey.

"Oh, man," he whispered unhappily. The

Pilgrims had worked so hard to get their food. They had had such a terrible winter—especially Priscilla. And now he had ruined their first Thanksgiving!

The door opened. Annie pulled Priscilla over to the hearth.

"See!" said Annie. "The turkey fell into the fire! It burned up!"

"I did it," Jack confessed.

Priscilla just stared at the burned turkey in the wet, messy hearth. Then she looked at Jack. He looked away from her.

"Ah, Jack," Priscilla said softly. "Thou looks sad."

He nodded.

"I ruined everything," he mumbled.

"No, thou did not," said Priscilla. She reached out her hand. "Come."

Priscilla led Jack and Annie out into the bright autumn light.

"Look," she said.

Jack saw Pilgrim women and kids walking to the tables. They all carried wooden platters piled with food.

"In the other houses, there was cooking also," said Priscilla.

Jack saw roasted ducks, turkeys, and deer meat. He saw baked fish, lobsters, eels, clams, and oysters.

He saw pumpkins, beans and corn, dried plums, berries and roasted nuts, steamy pots of soups and puddings, and loaves of baked breads.

"We had a very good harvest this fall," said Priscilla. "We stored many vegetables. We salted our fish and cured our meat. And today, our Wampanoag neighbors brought back five deer from the forest for our feast."

Jack was relieved to see all the food.

Priscilla knelt down and looked him in the eye.

"See, thou did not ruin anything, Jack," she said. "Thou and Annie have helped me a lot this day. You have both made me laugh. And you have both acted with kind hearts."

Jack was amazed. He thought he'd been no help at all.

"Come," said Priscilla. "Let us join the others. Art thou hungry?"

Jack nodded. Seeing all the platters of food had made him *really* hungry.

He and Annie followed Priscilla.

In the golden glow of autumn light, Jack and Annie joined the Pilgrims and the Wampanoag at the long tables.

Priscilla gave Jack and Annie wooden

plates. She gave them big white cloth napkins. Then she served them plenty of food.

Before they started to eat, Governor Bradford stood up to speak.

"Those of us who came here on the *Mayflower* did not know how to live in this land," he said. "But Squanto came to help us. And today, we give thanks for him, and for the peace we share with his people, and for all our great blessings."

Governor Bradford looked at Jack and Annie.

"Welcome to our feast," he said. "At this moment, three worlds—*your* world, *our* world, and the world of the Wampanoag—are not three. They are one. 'Tis the magic of community."

"Indeed!" said Annie. She clapped her hands and looked at Jack. "We did it," she whispered.

Did what? thought Jack.

Governor Bradford then put his napkin over his shoulder.

"Now!" he said. "Let us feast till our bellies are filled!"

As everyone started to eat, Annie leaned close to Jack.

"We found the special magic," she whispered. "The *magic of community*. Remember the rhyme?" She repeated Morgan's words:

"To find a special magic,
When work and toil are done,
Gather all together,
Turn three worlds into one."

"Oh, man," said Jack. He'd forgotten all about it.

"We can go home now," said Annie.

"No way," said Jack. "We have to eat first."

Jack and Annie used their fingers to pick

up their food. And they ate and ate and ate. Jack tried everything on his plate—except a little bit of eel and two clams. Everything he *did* eat, he liked—even the turnips.

Food really tastes good, he thought as he chewed, *when you eat it outside, on a beautiful day, with lots of nice people.*

9

Good Day

Slowly the feast came to an end. The guests wiped their plates with their last bits of bread. Then they wiped their hands and faces with their napkins.

Jack and Annie stood up.

"We have to go home," Annie said to Priscilla.

"Ah, thou must go back to thine own community now," said Priscilla.

Annie nodded. Then she kissed Priscilla on the cheek.

"Thanks for everything," Annie said.

Jack wanted to kiss Priscilla, too, but he was too shy.

"Thanks, Priscilla," he said.

"I thank *thee*, Jack," she said. Then she leaned over and kissed *his* cheek.

Jack felt his face grow red.

"Excuse me, sir," Annie said to Governor Bradford. "But we must leave now."

"Oh, but we have not yet taught thee how to grow corn!" said the little girl Mary.

Squanto stood up.

"Come," he said. "I will walk Jack and Annie back to the forest. I will teach them."

"Oh, thou does not have to do that," Jack said quickly. He feared that once they were alone, Squanto would figure out they'd never met before.

But Squanto only smiled and waited for them to follow.

"Bye, everyone!" said Annie, waving.

Jack waved, too. All the Pilgrims and Wampanoag waved back at them. The skinny dog barked.

Squanto led Jack and Annie away from the village toward the autumn woods. As they passed the cornfield, the dried stalks swayed in the breeze. They made *shushing* sounds.

Squanto stopped walking. He pointed to the field.

"You must plant corn in the spring," he said. "Put the seed in the ground when the oak-tree bud is as small as a mouse's ear."

"Oh, wait, please," said Jack. He slipped his notebook and pencil out of his bag. It was the first time he'd had a chance to take notes all day. He wrote:

How to Plant Corn:

oak-tree bud = mouse's ear

Then he looked up at Squanto and nodded.

"Dig holes and put two rotting fish in each hole," said Squanto.

"*Rotting fish?*" said Annie, making a face.

"Yes, rotting fish is good food for the soil," said Squanto. "On top of the fish, place four corn seeds. Then cover them with dirt."

Jack quickly wrote:

2 rotting fish, 4 corn seeds

Cover with dirt.

"Got it," he said, looking up.

"I give you these corn seeds to take

home," said Squanto. He held up a small pouch.

"Thanks," said Annie, taking the pouch.

"Thanks a lot," said Jack. "Well, good-bye." Jack was eager to get going—before Squanto could ask them questions about the past.

"Wait, I have a question," said Annie. "Squanto, why did you say you remembered us?"

Squanto's dark eyes twinkled. "I did not say I remembered *you*," he said. "I only said *I remember*."

"What did you remember?" asked Annie.

"I remembered what it was like to be from a different world," said Squanto. "Long ago, I lived with my people on this shore. But one day, men came in ships. They took me to

Europe as a slave. In that new land, I was a stranger. I felt different and afraid. I saw the same fear in your eyes today. So I tried to help you."

Annie smiled. "We thank thee," she said.

"And now *you* must always be kind to those who feel different and afraid," said Squanto. "Remember what you felt today."

"Indeed," said Jack.

Before closing his notebook, he added one last thing:

Be kind to those who feel
different and afraid.

Squanto bowed.

"Good day, Jack and Annie," he said.

"Good day!" they said.

Squanto turned and headed back to the village. The sun was setting. All of Plymouth was lit with a fiery light.

"It really was a good day," said Annie.

"Yeah, it was," said Jack.

Annie sighed. "Ready to go home?" she asked.

"Indeed," Jack said.

They started running through the woods.

Their feet crunched through the red and yellow leaves. They scrambled up the rope ladder into the tree house.

From the distance came the sounds of the Pilgrims singing a hymn and the Wampanoag beating their drums. Annie picked up the Pennsylvania book. She pointed at a picture of the Frog Creek woods.

"I wish we could go home!" she said.

"Good-bye, Priscilla!" Jack called.

"Good-bye, Squanto!" said Annie. "Good-bye, everyone!"

The wind started to blow.

The wind blew harder.

The tree house started to spin.

It spun faster and faster.

Then everything was still.

Absolutely still.

10

Thankful

Jack opened his eyes. He sighed. They were wearing their own clothes again. His leather bag was a backpack.

Sunlight slanted through the tree house window. As always, no time at all had passed in Frog Creek.

"Home," said Annie. She held up the pouch of corn seeds. "Proof for Morgan we found a special magic."

"The magic of community," said Jack.

Annie placed the pouch on the floor—next to the scrolls from Shakespeare and the twig from the gorillas of the cloud forest.

"Let's go," she said.

Jack took the research book out of his pack. He left it under the window. Then they climbed down the rope ladder.

As they started through the woods, a warm wind blew, rattling the leaves. Jack felt happy. He was looking forward to visiting their grandmother today and seeing their cousins and aunts and uncles.

"You know, Pilgrim kids had a really hard life," said Annie.

"Yeah. They did as much work as the grown-ups," said Jack. "Maybe more."

"Worst of all, lots of their friends and family members died," said Annie.

"Yeah," said Jack.

Both were silent for a moment.

"If *they* could be so thankful," said Annie, "*we* should be really thankful."

"No kidding," said Jack. "Really, *really* thankful."

And they were.

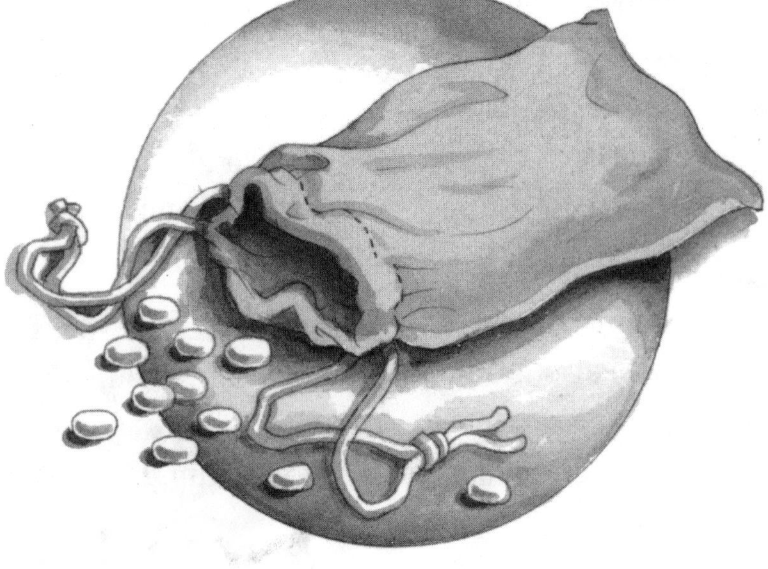

MORE FACTS FOR JACK AND ANNIE AND *YOU*!

In 1863, President Abraham Lincoln designated the last Thursday in November as a national day of Thanksgiving. But in 1939, President Franklin D. Roosevelt changed it to the fourth Thursday in November—in case there were ever five Thursdays in the month.

Wampanoag means "people of the first light." When the Pilgrims arrived, the Wampanoag people had lived in southeastern New England for thousands of years. They were experts at hunting, fishing, and planting.

Squanto's real name was Tisquantum. He was

a native of the Patuxet people, which belonged to the Wampanoag federation of tribes. The Patuxet had lived in Plymouth before the Pilgrims arrived. But when Squanto returned to Plymouth in 1619 after being kidnapped as a slave, he discovered that all his people had died in a plague in 1617. Since Squanto knew English as well as the language of the Wampanoag, he helped negotiate a peace treaty between the Pilgrims and Chief Massasoit.

Less than half of the original Pilgrims survived their first terrible winter. But after that, their numbers began to grow. More and more people came from England. Within ten years, the population of Plymouth Colony rose to almost 2,000.

Priscilla Mullins was the eighteen-year-old daughter of a shopkeeper. In the "general sickness" of the first year, she lost her parents and her brother. In 1623, Priscilla married another Pilgrim—John Alden, a barrel-maker. Priscilla and John had ten children.

The character of Mary was based on Mary Allerton, who was a small child when the Pilgrims landed in Plymouth. She was the last survivor of the *Mayflower*'s passengers. She died at Plymouth in 1699, at the age of eighty-three.

Don't miss the next Magic Tree House book, when Jack and Annie journey to old Hawaii and ride the waves in . . .

MAGIC TREE HOUSE® #28

HIGH TIDE IN HAWAII

March 2003

*Also Available on audio from Listening Library, read by Mary Pope Osborne!

Where have *you* traveled in the MAGIC TREE HOUSE®?

#1–4: The Mystery of the Tree House*

- ❑ **#1 Dinosaurs Before Dark** Jack and Annie find the tree house and travel to the time of dinosaurs.
- ❑ **#2 The Knight at Dawn** Jack and Annie go to the time of knights and explore a castle.
- ❑ **#3 Mummies in the Morning** Jack and Annie go to ancient Egypt and get lost in a pyramid while helping a ghost queen.
- ❑ **#4 Pirates Past Noon** Jack and Annie travel back in time and meet pirates with a treasure map.

#5–8: The Mystery of the Magic Spell*

- ❑ **#5 Night of the Ninjas** Jack and Annie go to old Japan and learn the secrets of the ninjas.
- ❑ **#6 Afternoon on the Amazon** Jack and Annie go to the Amazon rain forest and are greeted by army ants, crocodiles, and flesh-eating piranhas.
- ❑ **#7 Sunset of the Sabertooth** Jack and Annie go back to the Ice Age—the world of woolly mammoths, sabertooth tigers, and a mysterious sorcerer.
- ❑ **#8 Midnight on the Moon** Jack and Annie go *forward* in time and explore the moon.

#9–12: The Mystery of the Ancient Riddles*

- ❑ **#9 Dolphins at Daybreak** Jack and Annie take a mini-submarine into the world of sharks and dolphins.

- ❑ **#10 Ghost Town at Sundown** Jack and Annie travel to the Wild West, where they battle horse thieves, meet a kindly cowboy, and get help from a ghost.
- ❑ **#11 Lions at Lunchtime** Jack and Annie go to the plains of Africa, where they help wild animals cross a rushing river and have a picnic with a Masai warrior.
- ❑ **#12 Polar Bears Past Bedtime** Jack and Annie go to the Arctic, where they meet a seal hunter, play with polar bear cubs, and get trapped on thin ice.

#13–16: The Mystery of the Lost Stories*

- ❑ **#13 Vacation Under the Volcano** Jack and Annie land in Pompeii during Roman times, on the very day Mount Vesuvius erupts!
- ❑ **#14 Day of the Dragon King** Jack and Annie travel back to ancient China, where they must face an emperor who burns books.

- ❑ **#15 VIKING SHIPS AT SUNRISE** Jack and Annie visit a monastery in medieval Ireland on the day the Vikings attack!
- ❑ **#16 HOUR OF THE OLYMPICS** Jack and Annie go back to ancient Greece and the first Olympic games.

#17–20: The Mystery of the Enchanted Dog*

- ❑ **#17 TONIGHT ON THE TITANIC** Jack and Annie travel back to the decks of the *Titanic* and help two children escape from the sinking ship.
- ❑ **#18 BUFFALO BEFORE BREAKFAST** Jack and Annie go back in time to the Great Plains, where they meet a Lakota boy and stop a buffalo stampede!
- ❑ **#19 TIGERS AT TWILIGHT** Jack and Annie are whisked to a forest in India, where they are stalked by a hungry tiger!
- ❑ **#20 DINGOES AT DINNERTIME** Jack and Annie go to Australia and help a baby kangaroo and a koala bear escape from a wildfire.

#21–24: The Mystery of Morgan's Library*

- ❑ **#21 Civil War on Sunday** Jack and Annie go back in time to the War Between the States and help a famous nurse named Clara Barton.
- ❑ **#22 Revolutionary War on Wednesday** Jack and Annie go to the shores of the Delaware River the night George Washington and his troops prepare for their famous crossing!
- ❑ **#23 Twister on Tuesday** Jack and Annie help save students in a frontier schoolhouse when a tornado hits.
- ❑ **#24 Earthquake in the Early Morning** Jack and Annie go to San Francisco in 1906—just as the famous earthquake is shaking things up!

#25–28: The Mystery of Morgan's Rhymes

- ❑ **#25 STAGE FRIGHT ON A SUMMER NIGHT** Jack and Annie travel to Elizabethan England and help William Shakespeare put on a play.
- ❑ **#26 GOOD MORNING, GORILLAS** Jack and Annie go to the mountains of Africa and meet a family of gorillas!

A STEPPING STONE BOOK™

Great authors write great books . . .
for fantastic first reading experiences!

Grades 1–3

Duz Shedd series
by Marjorie Weinman Sharmat
Junie B. Jones series by Barbara Park
Magic Tree House® series
by Mary Pope Osborne
Marvin Redpost series by Louis Sachar

Clyde Robert Bulla
The Chalk Box Kid
The Paint Brush Kid
White Bird

J. C. Greenburg
#1 Andrew Lost on the Dog
#2 Andrew Lost in the Bathroom

Jackie French Koller
Mole and Shrew Are Two
Mole and Shrew All Year Through
Mole and Shrew Have Jobs to Do
Mole and Shrew Find a Clue

Jerry Spinelli
Tooter Pepperday
Blue Ribbon Blues: A Tooter Tale

Grades 2–4

A to Z Mysteries® series by Ron Roy
The Katie Lynn Cookie Company series
by G. E. Stanley

Adèle Geras
Little Swan

Stephanie Spinner & Jonathan Etra
Aliens for Breakfast
Aliens for Lunch
Aliens for Dinner

Gloria Whelan
Next Spring an Oriole
Silver
Hannah
Night of the Full Moon
Shadow of the Wolf

NONFICTION
Magic Tree House® Research Guid
by Will Osborne and
Mary Pope Osborne

Grades 3–5

The Magic Elements Quartet
by Mallory Loehr
#1: Water Wishes
#2: Earth Magic
#3: Wind Spell
#4: Fire Dreams

Spider Kane Mysteries
by Mary Pope Osborne
#1: Spider Kane and the Mystery Under the May-Apple
#2: Spider Kane and the Mystery at Jumbo Nightcrawler's

NONFICTION
Thomas Conklin
The *Titanic* Sinks!

Elizabeth Cody Kimmel
Balto and the Great Race

Look for these other books
by Mary Pope Osborne!

Picture books:
The Brave Little Seamstress
Kate and the Beanstalk
Moonhorse
New York's Bravest
Rocking Horse Christmas

For middle-grade readers:
Adaline Falling Star
American Tall Tales
The Deadly Power of Medusa
Favorite Greek Myths
Favorite Medieval Tales
Favorite Norse Myths
The Life of Jesus in Masterpieces of Art
Mermaid Tales from Around the World
One World, Many Religions
Spider Kane and the Mystery Under the May-Apple (#1)
Spider Kane and the Mystery at Jumbo Nightcrawler's (#2)
Standing in the Light

For young adult readers:
Haunted Waters